Parents and Caregivers,

Stone Arch Readers are designed to provide enjoyable reading experiences, as well as opportunities to develop vocabulary, literacy skills, and comprehension. Here are a few ways to support your beginning reader:

- Talk with your child about the ideas addressed in the story.

- Discuss each illustration, mentioning the characters, where they are, and what they are doing.

- Read with expression, pointing to each word. You may want to read the whole story through and then revisit parts of the story to ensure that the meanings of words or phrases are understood.

- Talk about why the character did what he or she did and what your child would do in that situation.

- Help your child connect with characters and events in the story.

Remember, reading with your child should be fun, not forced. Each moment spent reading with your child is a priceless investment in his or her literacy life.

Gail Saunders-Smith, Ph.D

STONE ARCH **READERS**

are published by Stone Arch Books,
A Capstone Imprint
151 Good Counsel Drive, P.O. Box 669
Mankato, Minnesota 56002
www.capstonepub.com

Library of Congress Cataloging-in-Publication Data
Suen, Anastasia.
     The scary night : a Robot and Rico story / by Anastasia Suen ; illustrated by
Mike Laughead.
     p. cm. – (Stone Arch readers)
     ISBN 978-1-4342-1628-1 (library binding)
     ISBN 978-1-4342-1752-3 (pbk.)
     [1. Camping–Fiction. 2. Robots–Fiction.] I. Laughead, Mike, ill. II. Title.
PZ7.S94343Sc 2010
[E]–dc22

                                                            2009000882

Summary: Robot and Rico are off on another adventure. This time they are going
camping. See if they make it through the night or if they get too scared.

Art Director: Bob Lentz
Graphic Designer: Hilary Wacholz

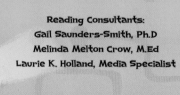

Reading Consultants:
Gail Saunders-Smith, Ph.D
Melinda Melton Crow, M.Ed
Laurie K. Holland, Media Specialist

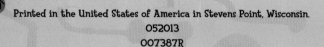

Printed in the United States of America in Stevens Point, Wisconsin.
052013
007387R

THE SCARY NIGHT

A ROBOT AND RICO STORY

BY ANASTASIA SUEN
ILLUSTRATED BY MIKE LAUGHEAD

STONE ARCH BOOKS
MINNEAPOLIS   SAN DIEGO

This is ROBOT.
Robot has lots of
tools. He uses the
tools to help his
best friend, Rico.

 Teapot

 Wings

 Scissors

 Fire Finger

 Special Shoes

 Roller Skates

"This is a good spot," says Rico.

"I'll put up the tent," says
Robot.

"I'll find wood," says Rico.
"Then we can make a fire."

"And eat," says Robot.

"This goes here," says Robot.
"And that goes there. Done."

"I have wood for a fire," says Rico.

Robot starts the fire. Robot and
Rico cook their hot dogs.

"It's dark in the woods,"
says Robot.

"I can tell a story," says Rico.

"What kind of story?" asks Robot.

"A scary story," says Rico.

"Oh," says Robot.

"In the deep dark woods," says
Rico, "there is a monster."

"The monster is big and hairy," says Rico.

"Oh, scary," says Robot.

"His name is Big Foot," says
Rico. "He has really big feet."

"The monster only comes out at night," says Rico.

"Why?" asks Robot.

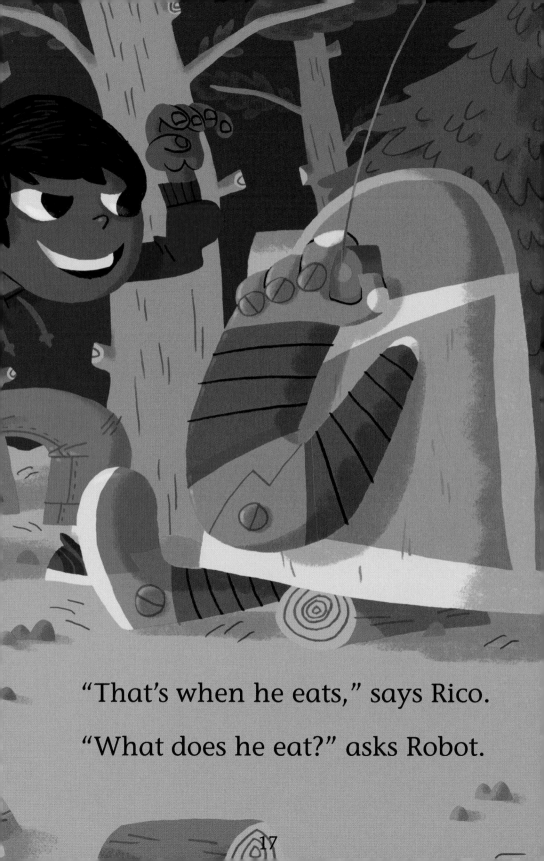

"That's when he eats," says Rico.

"What does he eat?" asks Robot.

"Everything," says Rico.

"Wow," says Robot.

"Big Foot hides in the trees,"
says Rico. "Then he jumps!"

"That is a scary story," says Robot.

"The fire is out," says Rico.
"We can go to sleep now."

Robot and Rico go into the tent.
They hear a loud noise. Snap!

"It's Big Foot!" says Rico.

Robot turns on his light.

"It's just a mouse," says Rico.

Crack!

Robot turns off his light. They hear another loud noise. Crack!

"It's Big Foot!" says Rico.

Robot turns on his light.

"It's just a rabbit," says Rico.

Robot turns off his light. They hear
another loud noise. Whoooo!

"It's Big Foot!" says Rico.

Robot turns on his light.

"It's just an owl," says Rico.

"Robot, can you please leave
the light on?" asks Rico.

"Sure," says Robot.

"Good night, Rico," says Robot.

"Good night, Robot," says Rico.

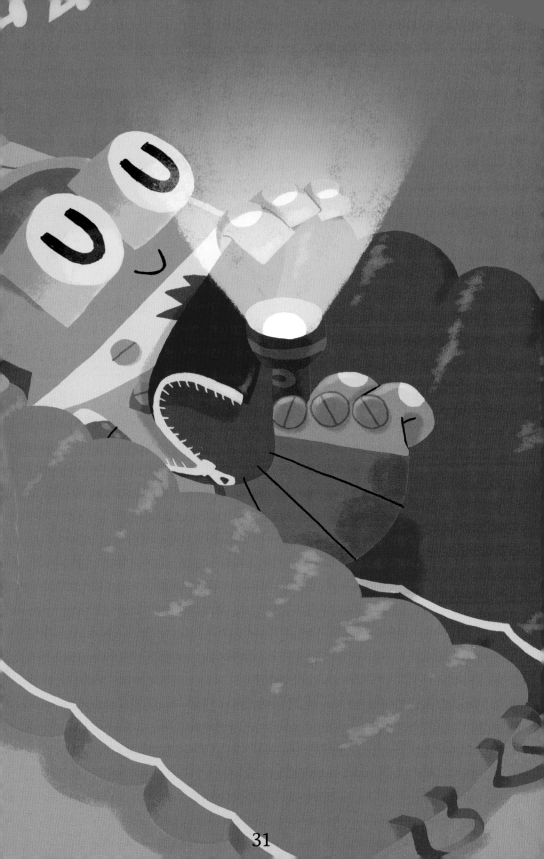

STORY WORDS

tent	fire	monster
wood	scary	light

Total Word Count: 341

One robot. One boy. One crazy fun friendship! Read all four Robot and Rico adventures!